THE ADVENTURE OF THE LICHFIELD MURDER

What Are People Saying About Sherlock Holmes' Adventures In Hugh Ashton's Books?

"Hundreds of Holmes pastiches, ranging in quality from godawful to brilliant, arc published every year. A few pastiche writers – Nicholas Meyer, June Thomson and Hugh Ashton, for example – sometimes are good enough to make you forget you're not reading the Master himself, having Watson narrate a lost but newly discovered story from some secret bank box or barrister's drawer." *Dallas Morning News, 19 December 2014*

"Hugh Ashton maintains his place as one of the best writers of new Sherlock Holmes stories, in both plotting and style." *(The District Messenger, newsletter of the Sherlock Holmes Society of London)*

" ...I would offer Hugh's own dialogue between Holmes and Watson after Sherlock displays his expertise at deducing details of a client's life before ever meeting them. Watson says, "You make it sound absurdly simple." Holmes replies, "It is indeed absurdly simple, and yet I seem to be the only man in London—nay, in the whole kingdom—who seems capable of the feat".

"Based on the number of authors who try and the few that succeed, Hugh Ashton makes something incredibly difficult look easy, and he "seems to be the only man in the whole kingdom capable of the feat"." *Dr. Philip C. Eyster, Consulting Sherlockian*

THE ADVENTURE OF
THE LICHFIELD
MURDER

FEATURING THE CELEBRATED CONSULTING DETECTIVE
MR. SHERLOCK HOLMES

AND RELATED BY
JOHN H. WATSON M.D.

DISCOVERED AND EDITED BY
HUGH ASHTON

J-VIEWS PUBLISHING, LICHFIELD, UK

The Adventure of the Lichfield Murder: Featuring the celebrated consulting detective Mr. Sherlock Holmes

Hugh Ashton

ISBN-13: 978-1-912605-01-9

ISBN-10: 1-912605-01-5

Published by j-views Publishing, 2018

The story entitled "The Lichfield Murder" first appeared in *The MX Book of New Sherlock Holmes Stories - Part I: 1881-1889,* pub. 2015

www.221BeanBakerStreet.info

j-views Publishing

26 Lombard Street, Lichfield, WS13 6DR, UK

www.j-views.biz

publish@j-views.biz

NOTE BY DR. WATSON

The case of Henry Staunton, in which my friend Sherlock Holmes became involved, was one of the more remarkable crimes of that year, though the true story never reached the ears of the public. Holmes himself expressed his wish that I should withhold the details until such occasion as he considered the time to be ripe. Since that occasion never transpired, I have kept the details in my dispatch-box, safe from the curious eyes of the present, but where they may possibly be discovered by generations and readers as yet unborn. Here, then, I present the remarkable events that transpired in the city of Lichfield in the year 188–.

Note: Originally, I used pseudonyms to denote the personalities and locations of this case, but have restored the originals, all the principals now being deceased.

"WE ALIGHTED FROM THE TRAIN AT LICHFIELD TRENT
VALLEY STATION, A MILE OR SO FROM THE CENTRE OF
THE CITY, AND HAILED A CAB TO TAKE US TO THE MARKET
SQUARE. FROM THERE, WE WALKED ALONG DAM-STREET UNTIL
WE REACHED NUMBER 23, CLOSE TO THE CATHEDRAL."

T the time that the events of which I am writing began, Sherlock Holmes was unengaged on any case. He had recently returned from the Continent, where he had been occupied with a matter of some delicacy regarding the ruling family of one of the minor German principalities, and now found time to hang idle on his hands.

He was amusing himself by attempting to discover a link between the Egyptian hieroglyphic system of writing, and that of the ancient peoples of the central American continent. This attempt, incidentally, proved to be fruitless, and the results of his researches never saw the light of day.

The rain was falling, and few cabs and even fewer pedestrians were on the street, as I stood in the window of our rooms in Baker-street observing the scene below.

"Halloa!" exclaimed Holmes, who had laid down his pen with a gesture of impatience, and joined me at the window. "A client, if I am not mistaken."

The corpulent man approaching our house certainly seemed to bear all the distinguishing marks of those who sought the assistance of Sherlock Holmes. The vacillation in his movements, and the nervous glances at the numbers displayed on the front doors of the houses of Baker-street had by now become almost as familiar to me as they were to Holmes.

As we watched, he glanced upwards, and caught sight of us standing in the window, as we in turn observed him. Hurriedly ducking his head downwards, he quickened his pace, half-running to the door, and within a matter of seconds we heard the pealing of the bell.

We returned to our seats as Mrs. Hudson announced

the arrival of our visitor, presenting Holmes with his card.

"A somewhat uninspiring choice of name," he announced, after examining the card, briefly presenting it to his long aquiline nose, and presenting it to me, where I read simply the name "Henry Taylor" and the title "Merchant". "No matter," he continued, "the truth will eventually come out. Show him up if you would, Mrs. Hudson."

The man who presented himself a few minutes later was clearly in the grip of a powerful emotion, in which fear appeared to be mingled with grief.

"Sit down, please, Mr. Taylor," Holmes invited him. "You have come far today, and no doubt you are tired."

"Why yes, Mr. Holmes, indeed I am." The words were uttered in an accent that betrayed our visitor as hailing from one of our more northern counties. He seated himself in the armchair usually occupied by Holmes' clients, and I was able to observe him more closely.

Clad in a tweed suit, more fitted for the country than the town, his large frame was still heaving with the exertion of having climbed the seventeen steps to our rooms, and to my professional eye, this, combined with his over-ruddy complexion, indicated some problems with his health. His left hand gripped a stout blackthorn, and the corner of a sheaf of papers peeked out from beneath his coat. His eyes were reddened, as though he had been weeping.

"Forgive my impertinence," Holmes said to him after about a minute had passed in silence, "but is your visit here connected with your recent loss?"

I myself had, naturally, remarked the mourning

band attached to his right sleeve.

For answer, Taylor raised his head, which had sunk to his breast, and answered in a lugubrious tone, "Yes, Mr. Holmes, that is indeed the case." Another silence ensued, broken only by the wheezing emanating from our visitor as he slowly regained his composure. At length, he spoke again, in a voice heavily charged with emotion. "Gone, Mr. Holmes. Gone. Struck down in the full flower of her beauty by a fell hand."

"Murder, you say?" exclaimed Holmes in a tone of some excitement. The news seemed to arouse him from his languor. "How very fortuitous— I mean to say that it is fortuitous that I have no other cases on hand, of course. The police...?"

"The police have their suspicions as to who may have committed this foul crime, but I believe them to be in error," replied the other. "This is why I have come to you. I wish to seek justice for my dear wife Martha."

"Tell me more," Holmes invited him, leaning back in his chair and regarding our client with that curious hooded gaze of his. "Watson, take notes, if you would be so kind."

"I am a merchant of cloth and other such goods," began our visitor. "Some years ago, my first wife died of consumption, leaving me with two young children. As a busy man of business, I found I was unable to care for them as they deserved, and I thereupon lodged them with my sister in the town of Burton upon Trent, and made due financial provision for their support. Though my sister is a good woman, and took excellent care of them, I nonetheless felt that my children deserved to be with their father and his wife. In addition, living alone was irksome to me, and I therefore cast about for a wife. When I moved to the city where I currently reside, my eye was caught by Martha Lightfoot, the daughter of a neighbour, and after a brief courtship, we married, and my children, Stephen and Katie, returned to my home." He paused, and I took the opportunity to offer him a glass of water, which he accepted gratefully. "Well, sir, it seemed I could not have made a better choice for a wife. Martha was devoted to my children as if they had been her own, and they, for their part, appeared to adore her in return."

"Excuse me," Holmes interrupted him. "May I ask the ages of the principals in this case?"

Our visitor smiled, for the first time since he had entered our room. "I suppose that some would term our marriage – our late marriage, that is – a December and May affair. When we married, some two years ago, I was fifty-three years of age, and Martha twenty-two. Stephen was at that time twelve years old, and Katie ten." He paused and mopped his brow with a none-too-clean handkerchief. "We were a happy family, in so far as my work would allow it."

"What do you mean by that?" Holmes asked him sharply.

"Well, Mr. Holmes, my work involves a good deal of travel, and obliges me to be away from home for considerable periods of time. I considered it to be somewhat of an imposition on Martha for her to care alone for two youngsters, but as I mentioned, she and the children appeared to have a harmonious life together. That is," he sighed, "until the events of a month ago."

"Pray continue," Holmes requested, as our visitor seemed to have sunk into some kind of reverie.

"I came back from an extended trip that had lasted for a week, and discovered my Stephen in an uncharacteristically sulky mood, and with what appeared to be a bruise upon his face. I assumed that he had received a blow while scuffling with his playfellows, as lads will, but on my questioning him, he informed me that the blow had been struck by my wife. He refused to give the reason for this event, simply referring me to Martha. When I questioned her, and confronted her with the accusation, she admitted to striking the child, but claimed it had not been a deliberate action."

"No doubt she was able to give reasons for this assertion?"

Taylor sighed. "Yes. She informed me that she had observed Stephen taking money from the maid's purse. A small sum, to be sure – a few pence only – but theft is theft, no matter what the amount, do you not agree, Mr. Holmes?"

"Indeed so," answered my friend, with a half-smile.

"She remonstrated with him, and an argument ensued, during the course of which she attempted to retrieve the money, and struck the lad in the face. She swore to me with tears in her eyes that it was an accident, and she had never had any intention of doing him harm. He, when I questioned him later, admitted that he had taken the money in order to purchase some trifle, but claimed that Martha had deliberately delivered the blow to his face."

"And which one did you believe?"

Taylor sighed. "I believed my wife, Martha. Much as I love my Stephen, he has proved himself to be less than truthful in the past, and I have had cause to admonish him. I fear that the sojourn at my sister's did nothing to improve his character. She is a woman whom some might term over-kind, and she indulged his whims while he was living there, at the expense of his character."

"I take it that relations between your wife and your son deteriorated from that time?"

"Indeed so, Mr. Holmes. As I mentioned, I am often compelled to be away from home, and so it was for this past month. However, on recent occasions when I returned from my travels, it was painfully obvious to me that my wife and my son were on poor terms with each other. I confess that I was completely ignorant of any way in which this breach could be mended, and was forced to endure the spectacle of those whom I love in a state of mutual enmity. Mealtimes were a particular torment, where each seemed to find every opportunity to insult and belittle the other. If one could be banished from the table, peace would have prevailed, and as master of the house, I could remove one of the sources of conflict. But which one was to be removed, Mr. Holmes? I ask you, for I could not resolve that riddle." He paused, as if for effect. "And then, Mr. Holmes, we come to the events of yesterday."

"It was last night that your wife died?"

"Indeed it was only yesterday. I returned home to find Martha lifeless, stretched out in her own blood on the drawing-room floor. She had suffered a series of stab wounds to the body."

"And your son?"

"I discovered him in the scullery, with a bloody kitchen knife. He was cleaning bloodstains off his clothes in an almost frantic manner. The water in the basin in which he was washing his hands and garments was a scarlet mess, Mr. Holmes. I never want to see the like again."

"And his story?"

"He told me that he had discovered my Martha in the room, with the knife beside her. Despite his recent dislike of her, he is not at heart a bad lad. He believed that she was not dead, but severely wounded, and attempted to move her to make her more comfortable. It was during this operation that he determined that she was in fact dead, and it was at this time that his hands and clothing became covered in blood. He picked up the knife—"

"Why did he do that?" I asked.

Taylor shrugged. "Who can tell?"

"The mind causes us to act strangely and without rational motive under unusual conditions," remarked Holmes. "I can think of several similar cases in my experience. Go on, Mr. Taylor."

"He picked up the knife, as I say, and carried it with him into the scullery, where he started to wash his hands and to clean the blood from his clothes. When I encountered him, I immediately ordered him to cease what he was doing, and to come into the street with me, where I gave him over to a passing constable. It gave me little pleasure to do so, but I felt that justice must be served."

"Quite so, quite so," murmured Holmes, but his words seemed to me to lack conviction.

"I felt in my heart that it was impossible that he had committed such a base deed, but what other explanation could be given?"

"You mentioned a maid," said Holmes. "Where was she while this was going on?"

"It was her afternoon off."

"I see. And your daughter?"

"She was visiting a schoolfellow. My son and my

wife were the only two people in the house when I returned."

"When you returned, was the house door to the street locked?"

"The police asked me the same question. Yes, it was. The door leading to the back yard was also locked."

"And there was no sign of entry through any other aperture? A window, for example?"

"To the best of my knowledge, there was no such sign."

"And the police?"

Taylor spread his hands. "What can they do, but believe that my son is guilty? What other explanation could there possibly be for these events? They are confining him, and I fear he will hang."

"Even if he is guilty, it is not likely he will be hanged," Holmes informed him, not without a certain sympathy in his manner. "The courts often show clemency to younger offenders, even in the case of serious crimes. However, I take it you will wish me to establish his innocence?"

"Of course, Mr. Holmes. But may I ask your fee? I am not a wealthy man, and I fear that I may be unable to afford your services."

"My fees never vary, save on those occasions when I remit them altogether," smiled Holmes. He scribbled a few lines on a card and handed it to Taylor. "I advise you to return to Euston and take the fastest train available back to Lichfield. Do you happen to know the name of the police agent in charge of the case?"

Taylor started at Holmes' pronouncement of the name of the Midlands city, and appeared somewhat dumbfounded at this exhibition of my friend's deductive powers, but confined his speech to answering the question put to him. "An Inspector Upton, I believe, of the Staffordshire Constabulary."

"Excellent. Pray give him this message, and inform him that I will be arriving soon. Thank you, Mr. Taylor. We will join you at your house. Where may we find it?"

"Dam-street, on the way from the marketplace to the Cathedral. Number 23."

"We will find it, never fear."

Our visitor picked up his hat, and bidding us farewell, departed.

I turned to Holmes in astonishment. "How on earth did you know that he lived in Lichfield?"

"Elementary. When I see that not only his hat bears the label of a tailor in that city, but that his stick also bears the mark of a merchant there, I am forced to conclude that most of his purchases are made in Lichfield. Since he describes himself as a merchant who travels extensively, I consider it unlikely that he lives in a village, since Lichfield is a city well served by two railway stations. Lichfield therefore presents itself to me as his city of residence. In addition, today's weather being wet, I would have expected his boots and his stick to display splashes of mud if he lived outside the city. It is obvious, therefore, since they did not display such signs, that his journey on foot was conducted along paved thoroughfares. Hence my conclusion that he lives in the city. It is, by the by," he added, "a city with which my family has some connection. An ancestor, one Joshua Holmes, is said to have been an intimate of Erasmus Darwin and Anna Seward, and occupied a handsome property in Lichfield close to the Cathedral Close. Family lore has it that he engaged in the same line of business as do I." Holmes smiled.

"And you remarked that his name was uninspired. Surely a man has no choice regarding his name."

"Under certain circumstances, he may well be able to choose," answered Holmes, but did not expound further on this somewhat enigmatic pronouncement. "Did you not remark that the card he presented to us still smells strongly of printer's ink, thereby signifying that it has been produced very recently? Not only that, but the initials marked in ink inside the hat were not HT, but HS? Mr. Taylor, or whatever his true name may be, does not strike one as the kind of man who borrows others' hats."

"You see more than I do," I remarked.

"On the contrary, Watson, you see all that I do. I merely draw logical inferences from what I see, and you fail to do so."

"And those papers he was carrying inside his coat. What were they? I had assumed that they had some relevance to his query."

"I, too," confessed Holmes. "Many of them appeared to be letters, from the little I could observe, and I fancy that at least one of them was a will."

"His late wife's?" I asked. Holmes shrugged.

"Who can tell with certainty? But we may assume so, I think. In any case, we must move fast, before the heavy boots of the local constabulary remove all traces of evidence from the scene. As you know, I have little faith in the abilities of our Metropolitan Police, and even less in those of the provincial forces." He rang the bell for Billy, our page, and wrote and handed him another note, to be sent as a telegram to the police inspector in Lichfield.

"You are prepared to stay in the Midlands for a few days?"

"It is the work of a minute for me to be ready," I answered him.

"Good. If I recall correctly, there is an express train from Euston at fifty-three minutes past the hour, which will bring us to the Trent Valley station before the day is too far advanced. Be so good as to confirm it in Bradshaw."

I did so, and reported this to Holmes. "I confess that I am confused regarding our client's motives," I said to Holmes. "On the one hand, he appears to love his son with true parental feeling by approaching you in an attempt to establish his innocence. On the other, he seems keen to blacken his name, as shown by his confession that the child is not always truthful. Also, by immediately giving his son in charge to the police, Taylor seems to have assumed that he was indeed the culprit, without bothering to make detailed enquiries."

"Indeed, there are several mysteries about this aspect of the matter, which I think we can only clear up by means of a visit to the scene. Come, Watson, let us make our way to the fair city of Lichfield."

 E alighted from the train at Lichfield Trent Valley station, a mile or so from the centre of the city, and hailed a cab to take us to the market square. From there, we walked along Dam-street until we reached number 23, close to the Cathedral. A police constable was standing outside the door.

Holmes introduced himself to the constable, and requested permission to speak to the Inspector in charge of the case.

"I've read of you in the newspapers, sir," replied the policeman, "and I am sure that you will be welcome, but I have to talk to Inspector Upton first before I allow you inside, if you don't mind, sir." He went inside the house, and re-emerged a minute or so later, followed by a uniformed officer, who identified himself as the inspector.

"Mr. Holmes, sir, welcome to Lichfield. A pleasure to make your acquaintance, though I fear there will be not much for you to do here. We are pretty certain that the young 'un is the culprit."

"You received my telegram?" Holmes asked him.

"Why, yes sir, we did indeed, and Taylor has presented your card to me. You'll be happy to know that the room is not significantly changed from when Taylor entered it and discovered his wife there, though of course we have removed the body. As I say, there is really no doubt that the lad did it. Shocking case. I can't remember anything like this happening here in the past. This way, sir."

He led the way into the front room of the house, which had been furnished in a good, if provincial style. Holmes stood in the doorway, and surveyed the room's contents, which included a desk by the window, and a chair lying on its side beside it. Some dark stains marked the carpet and the bearskin rug beside the desk.

"The front and back doors of the house were both locked, Taylor told us," we were informed by Upton. "All the windows appeared to be shut, and there was no other means of entrance into the house."

"Unless the murderer came down the chimney, or through the coal-chute, assuming there to be such a thing in this house."

"True enough, Mr. Holmes, as regards the coal-chute, but no such apparatus exists here."

"The case against the boy certainly seems strong, then."

"Strong enough, Mr. Holmes. It's a pity, as he seems like a nice lad. Just a sudden flash of temper, and—" The inspector shrugged.

"Where was the body located?" Holmes asked.

By way of answer, the police officer started to step forward to point out the spot, but was restrained by Holmes. "Please, Inspector," he implored the other, "let us not disturb any further the remaining evidence that will help us determine the murderer, faint as it may be by now."

"Very well, then," replied Upton. "Mrs. Taylor was discovered by Taylor lying on her back, over there by the desk, with her head nearest the chair."

"And yet she had been sitting at the desk, had she not, and the chair was overturned in the struggle with her murderer," mused Holmes to himself. "Strange. Taylor told me that the son, Stephen, had moved the body, but did not provide any details," addressing the policeman once more. "Do you know more?"

"According to the son's statement, he discovered his mother – rather, his step-mother – lying on her side, and merely moved her onto her back, and at that time determined that she was dead."

"I see," said Holmes. "And where was the knife discovered, according to this statement?"

"Beside the body, on the floor."

Holmes said nothing, but stood in silence for a moment before dropping to his hands and knees, and pulling out a lens from his pocket, with which he proceeded to examine the floor, crawling forward towards the desk as he did so. At one point he paused, and appeared to be about to retrieve something from the rug, but checked his movements and continued his appraisal of the carpet. The policeman and I watched him from the doorway for the space of about five minutes.

At length he stood up, and dusted his garments, before turning to the desk and using his lens to scrutinise its surface, and the inkwell which still stood open, as well as the pen and the blotter and other objects that lay upon it. "Your men have been busy," he said to Upton, "and have almost, but not completely, destroyed the traces of the events that took place. Nonetheless, many points of interest still remain. May we view the body of Mrs. Taylor?"

"She is at a local inn, the Earl of Lichfield Arms, in Conduit-street by the market square," replied the inspector. "Though I fail to see that there is much to be learned from a further examination."

"There may well be more than you imagine," answered my friend. "May I advise you that no-one is to enter this room until I have finished my investigation?"

I could see that the police officer resented this usurpation of his authority, but he assented to Holmes' request, and instructed the constable at the door to prevent any entrance to the chamber.

The inspector accompanied Holmes and myself on the short walk to the inn, where we were shown to an upstairs room, which had been cleared of all furniture save a deal table on which lay the body, covered by a sheet.

"There has as yet been no autopsy, of course?"

Holmes enquired.

On receiving the information that this was the case, he requested and received permission to draw down the sheet and examine the body. There were several wounds to the abdomen, obviously inflicted with a sharp instrument.

"In my opinion," I said to Holmes, in answer to his query, "this wound here could well have reached the heart. Of course, without a post-mortem examination, it will be impossible to say with certainty that this is the case, but my experience with bayonet wounds leads me to this belief. Even without the other wounds, this alone could be the cause of death. Shock and loss of blood would also be a factor in the cause of death."

"Thank you, Watson," Holmes said. "As you rightly point out, this cannot be confirmed until an autopsy is performed, and it would be premature to certify this as the cause of death. But, dear me, this murder was committed in a frenzy of passion, was it not? I count at least five major wounds, and several grazes where the weapon has almost, but not completely, missed its mark." He bent to examine the ghastly wounds more closely. "Watson. Your opinion on the nature of these? Specifically, how they were delivered."

I, in my turn, bent to the cadaver. "Delivered to the front of the body, with the blade entering from the right and above for the most part."

"That was also my conclusion," said Holmes. "Mrs. Taylor appears to have been quite a tall woman, Inspector. Can you confirm that?"

"I believe she was some five feet and seven inches in height." Holmes made some notes in his pocket note-book.

"And the boy?"

"He is somewhat small for his age. I would put him at a little under five feet."

"And it would take considerable strength, would it not, Watson, to cause these wounds?"

"Indeed so," I confirmed. Holmes bent to the body once more, and eventually stood straight and addressed Upton again.

"What was the state of the boy's mind when the constable took him in charge, Inspector?"

"According to the constable's report, he was shaking. The constable judged him to be in a state of fear."

"That is hardly surprising," Holmes commented. "And he has not confessed to the murder?"

"He continues to insist that he entered the room and discovered his step-mother lying in her own blood. As to the knife, he says that he has no idea why he picked it up and carried it with him to the scullery where he washed his hands and clothing."

"Those in such a condition often are unaware of their actions," answered Holmes. "I think we may attach little importance to this. You are satisfied, of course, that the knife discovered with the boy is indeed the murder weapon?"

"Why, what else could it be?" asked Upton in surprise. "You may see it for yourself at the station. I take it you will wish to interview the boy?"

"If that is permitted."

"Surely," replied the inspector. "Though I fear you will be wasting your breath if you are attempting to establish his innocence."

"We shall see," answered Holmes. "By the by, where is Taylor now? He did not seem to be in evidence at the house."

"He has left the city for the day. He told me that he

had urgent business in Birmingham to which he must attend, and I allowed him to go there."

"I have a feeling that you may never again set eyes on Mr. Henry Taylor," Holmes told him.

"Why, what can you possibly mean?" asked Upton in surprise and dismay. "Do you mean that he means to do away with himself in despair? Have I let him go to his self-inflicted death?"

"By no means," smiled Holmes. "The truth will prove to be at once simpler and more complex than that."

"You have me scratching my head," said Upton in puzzlement, and led the way to the police station, where he produced for our inspection the knife that had been discovered by the body.

Holmes produced his lens, and examined the blade, covered with now-dried blood, closely. "It is impossible to say with any certainty without knowing the exact position and location of the knife when it was found," he announced at length, "but it seems to me that this knife was not the murder weapon. Has it been identified, by the way?"

"Yes, Taylor recognised it as one of the knives used in the kitchen for preparing food. The maid, Anne Hilton, likewise identified it, as indeed does the boy Stephen. But why do you say that it is not the murder weapon. Surely it is obvious?"

"Too obvious," retorted Holmes. "Two factors lead me to this conclusion, which, as I said, must remain tentative for now. Firstly, the blade, as you will observe, is almost triangular in shape, with a narrow point, and widening towards the hilt."

"That is a common design," answered Upton, "and I fail to see how you can make anything of that."

"Ah, but the wounds on the body were performed using a narrower blade. Either that, or this knife was not inserted to its full depth."

"In which case, it could not have reached the heart, as I surmised," I interrupted.

"Precisely, Watson," he confirmed. "And in that event also, the blade near the hilt would not have been coated with blood, at least not to the even degree that blade exhibits. To me, this has all the appearance of a knife that has been deliberately smeared with blood, possibly not even human blood, and left beside the body, while the actual murder weapon is still missing."

"But no other weapon was found in the room or indeed in the house," protested the policeman.

"And there was no-one else in the house other than the boy and his step-mother, according to the boy's story, and that of Taylor," Holmes added. "And the boy never left the house, it would appear."

"You continue to produce puzzles, Mr. Holmes. Do you wish to see the boy now?"

"Thank you, yes."

I will not dwell for long on the exchange between the poor child and Holmes. The boy was clearly in a wretched state, and though he freely admitted the bad feeling that had recently sprung up between him and his late step-mother, and confirmed the story that had been told to us by Taylor, he emphatically denied her murder. The only new detail he added that we had not previously heard was his account of having heard some noises, as of something heavy falling, a few minutes before he entered the drawing-room. He appeared to be a somewhat nervous youth, of somewhat slender build, and undersized for his age.

Holmes produced his notebook, and asked the lad

to draw a rough sketch of the room and the position of the body and the knife when he discovered them. Examining the diagram, he complimented the boy on his skills, for which he received a faint smile from the youth.

"And there were no papers on the desk or lying around the room?" he asked the boy by way of concluding the interview.

Stephen Taylor shook his head. "Nothing like that, sir," he answered.

"Thank you," Holmes told him. "I am confident," he added, to Upton's obvious astonishment, "that you will be out of here very soon."

"What in the world did you mean by raising the boy's hopes with false promises like that?" Upton asked Holmes, almost angrily, when we were walking back to the inspector's office. "That was indeed a cruel jest to play on the poor lad, was it not?"

"No jest," Holmes told him. "I believe that we can have this whole matter cleared up in a matter of hours. May I make a request that you send word to Sutton Coldfield police station, and ask them to send a Mr. Henry Staunton to you for questioning in connection with this matter? A house in Victoria Road, I believe, will find him."

"In the name of all that's good, Mr. Holmes!" exclaimed the policeman. "What on earth can you want with such a person? And how do you come to know of him?"

"I feel that he will be most germane to your enquiries," Holmes answered him. "As to how I have knowledge of him, why, the answer stood as clearly before you as it did to me."

"Very well. If this request had come from any other

source, I would have regarded it as the ravings of a madman, but your reputation, Mr. Holmes, precedes you, and I will do as you ask, though I fail to comprehend your reasoning on this matter."

"While we are awaiting the arrival of Mr. Henry Staunton," Holmes said to Upton, "we will find lodgings. I doubt if we will wish to be accommodated in the Earl of Lichfield Arms. I have heard the George spoken well of by an acquaintance who passed through this city once."

"The George is indeed a pleasant hostelry. I will send for you there once Staunton, whoever he may transpire to be, arrives here."

"Come, Watson," Holmes said to me, and we passed through the pleasant streets of this old city to the George, where we secured a most comfortable room, and bespoke an early dinner, anticipating the arrival of Staunton.

Over the course of our meal, I attempted to interrogate Holmes regarding what he had discovered, and the conclusions he had drawn, but much to my chagrin, he refused to be drawn, and discoursed instead on the life of Doctor Samuel Johnson, a native of the city that we were currently visiting. I could follow his reasoning with regard to the knife, and was forced to agree that the knife that had been discovered by the body was in all probability not the murder weapon. It also seemed to me that the boy was unable to have inflicted the wounds that had caused the death of Mrs. Taylor, by reason of his under-developed physique.

We had just finished our meal when a uniformed constable entered the dining-room, much to the consternation of the hotel waiters, and informed us, with a strange smile, that Mr. Henry Staunton from Sutton

Coldfield was now at Lichfield police station.

"Inspector Upton's compliments to you, Mr. Holmes," he added with a broad grin. "He thanks you for your discovery of Mr. Staunton, sir."

We followed the constable to the police station, where we encountered the inspector who wore the same smile as his constables. "Mr. Staunton is in the next room," he told us, and opened the door – to reveal Mr. Henry Taylor!

"What is the meaning of this?" I asked. "Are Henry Staunton and Henry Taylor one and the same person?"

"Indeed so."

Our client's face had turned red with anger. "How the devil did you discover all this?" he demanded of Holmes.

"You thought that by removing and destroying the letter that your second wife had written to your first wife, informing her of Mrs. Taylor's new-found knowledge of Mrs. Staunton, you had removed any possible evidence of a motive, did you not? But you failed to notice that she had blotted the envelope. Your true name and address were clearly visible on the blotter, reversed, naturally."

"My God!" Staunton sank back in his chair.

"Bigamy, eh?" said Upton. "Well, my lad, we can have you for that."

"And add to that the murder of Martha Taylor, as I suppose I must call her," said Holmes, "though I fear her actual marital status must be in some doubt."

"I never meant to kill her—" " cried Staunton, and bit off the words as they came out of his mouth.

"Oh, but I think you did indeed kill her, and then worse," said Holmes. "In my whole career, I have hardly ever encountered such a cold-hearted diabolical piece of treachery."

"Your proof?" taunted the other.

"It would be easy to prove to a jury that the blows that killed Martha Taylor were not inflicted by the knife found beside her body. The blows that killed her could only have been inflicted by a stiletto blade, as any wide blade would have been stopped by the ribs. Once that doubt had been established, your son would walk free. No other possible weapon was discovered in the house. You may have thought you were being clever by killing with one weapon and leaving another, more plausible instrument to implicate an innocent party – your very son – but you ignored elementary anatomy."

"That might prove my son's innocence, but it hardly establishes my guilt," protested Staunton defiantly.

"True," agreed Holmes. "However, there is the matter of the missing seal from your watch chain, the empty clasp of which I noticed when you visited us in Baker-street." Staunton looked aghast and grabbed at the chain in question with a look of horror on his countenance. "No, it did not fall off somewhere else. It is currently pressed into the bearskin rug in the front room of the house in Dam-street. Did your men overlook this, Inspector? Pressed in there by the weight of a body lying on it, and covered with blood. It is impossible that in that state it was ever positioned there after Martha Taylor was struck down.

Let me reconstruct the events for you, gentlemen. Mr. Staunton took a fancy to have more than one name, and more than one family. It happens to some men. I am myself not that way inclined, but I regard this aberration with an amused tolerance. As Mr.

Taylor, he was widowed, and he removed himself to Lichfield, where he cast about for a new partner. Mrs. Staunton is obviously not suited as the ideal sole help-meet and companion of his life—"

"Leave her out of this, damn you!" exclaimed Staunton, angrily.

"By all means," answered Holmes with an equable air. "In any event, Miss Martha Lightfoot fitted the bill, and she appears to have been a good match, and an excellent parent to the two children of the first Mrs. Taylor."

"The best," sighed Staunton, with what seemed to be genuine regret.

"But she became suspicious of her husband's frequent absences, which were not always as concerned with his supposed business as she had first thought. Somehow, perhaps by means of a private detective, or some other method, she discovered that her supposed beloved husband was maintaining another establishment in neighbouring Sutton Coldfield, and she decided to confront her husband with the knowledge. At this time, a coolness developed between her and Staunton's son.

"She told Staunton that she was about to reveal his double life, and confront his other wife with the knowledge of her existence. Frightened that he was about to be ruined, and quite possibly be prosecuted, for his duplicity, when he returned home and saw his wife writing at the desk, he immediately guessed what she was about. He quietly let himself into the house and went to the kitchen for a knife. Entering the drawing-room, he confronted his wife, who was indeed writing the fatal missive. A violent argument ensued, during which he produced the kitchen knife, and in defence, she snatched up the long paper-knife that lay in its holder on the desk. You really should have taken better note of that empty knife-holder, Inspector."

"Since we believed the murder weapon had already been discovered, it seemed to be of no importance," answered the abashed police agent.

"Well, well. Be that as it may. In the ensuing struggle, which took place in near-silence, the kitchen knife was dropped, and the stiletto paper-knife passed from Martha Taylor to Henry Staunton, who in his blind fury used it to kill the unfortunate woman. It was at about this time that the seal was ripped from the watch-chain. The fastening is twisted on both the chain, and the seal itself, and I have no doubt that you will easily find a perfect match there, Inspector.

"You will remember Doctor Watson's characterisation of the fatal wounds, and also note the fact that Staunton here is left-handed. His son is right-handed, as I ascertained when I asked him to sketch the scene of the murder. The wounds could only have been inflicted either by standing behind the victim and stabbing her by reaching over her shoulder, stabbing downwards – a most awkward way of delivering the blows, and one which is contradicted by the position of the body's head relative to the chair – or alternatively if the victim was standing, by stabbing with the murderer facing his victim, using an overhand grip – less effective, perhaps, than the underhand grip, but ultimately fatal. Am I correct so far, Staunton?" He received no answer, other than a silent, grim-faced nod, and continued.

"Being faced with the undisputed fact that he was now the killer of the woman with whom he shared his house, his principal object now was to avoid detection.

He quickly snatched up the fatal letter in its envelope, which had only just been addressed and blotted before he entered the room. He knew his son was in the house, and his twisted mind instantly conceived a way in which he could escape blame, and transfer it to his own flesh and blood."

"A foul and heinous act," growled Upton.

"He secreted the stiletto, and smeared the kitchen knife with blood before letting the chair fall with a crash, to alert the boy and to draw his attention, before letting himself out of the front door and silently re-locking it. He disposed of the murder weapon, and I have no doubt that if you drag the Minster Pool at the end where Dam-street runs close by, you will discover it there. The rest you know."

" I never meant to kill her!" wailed the unfortunate Staunton. "It was my intention only to prevent her from sending the letter."

"That's as may be," replied Inspector Upton in stony tones. "But instead of confessing to your guilt like a man, you attempted to fasten the crime on a poor defenceless young man – your own flesh and blood at that."

"I never meant him to go to the gallows," cried Staunton, in an agony of distress.

"Maybe you did not," answered the police agent. "But I will make every effort to ensure that you make that trip yourself. Thank you, Mr. Holmes. You have saved a young man's life, and prevented a grave miscarriage of justice."

"All I ask," replied Holmes, "is that my name not be mentioned in connection with this case. Inspector Upton shall take all the credit for the observations and deductions, and the bringing to justice of Mr.

Henry Staunton. Come, Watson, our task is done, and I think that we shall sleep well tonight at the George before our return to London on the morrow."

"But why in heaven's name," I could not refrain from asking Holmes as we made our way from the police station, "did Staunton ask you to clear the boy's name, given that this inevitably would lead to the proof of his own guilt?"

Holmes shook his head. "He believed that he had committed the perfect crime, and that suspicion would never fall on him," he said. "We may see his retaining me as an act of bravado and cocking a snook at the police. After all, who would believe that a man who had hired the foremost man in his field to clear his son's name would himself be guilty of any wrongdoing? Unfortunately for Mr. Henry Staunton, he underestimated my abilities, as have so many others in the past. It is their loss."

"And the world's gain," I added.

Holmes' only answer was his familiar sardonic smile.

ALSO BY HUGH ASHTON:

Beneath Gray Skies
Red Wheels Turning
At the Sharpe End
Tales of Old Japanese
Leo's Luck
Balance of Powers
The Untime
The Untime Revisited
Angels Unawares

SHERLOCK HOLMES TITLES:

Tales from the Deed Box of John H. Watson MD
More from the Deed Box of John H. Watson MD
Secrets from the Deed Box of John H. Watson MD
The Darlington Substitution
The Trepoff Murder
The Deed Box of John H. Watson MD
Notes from the Dispatch-Box of John H. Watson MD
Further Notes from the Dispatch-Box of John H. Watson MD
The Reigate Poisoning Case: Concluded
The Death of Cardinal Tosca
Without My Boswell
Last Notes from the Dispatch-Box of John H. Watson MD
1894
Some Singular Cases of Mr. Sherlock Holmes

FOR CHILDREN
(WITH ILLUSTRATIONS BY ANDY BOERGER):

Sherlock Ferret and the Missing Necklace
Sherlock Ferret and the Multiplying Masterpieces
Sherlock Ferret and the Poisoned Pond
The Adventures of Sherlock Ferret

COLOPHON

 E decided that this adventure of Sherlock Holmes deserved to be reproduced on paper in as authentic a fashion as was possible given modern technology.

Accordingly, after consulting the reproductions of the original Holmes adventures as printed in *The Strand Magazine*, we decided to use the Monotype Bruce Old Style font from Bitstream as the body (10 on 11.5). Though it would probably look better letterpressed than printed using a lithographic or laser method, and is missing old-style numerals, it still manages to convey the feel of the original. The flowers are Bodoni Ornaments, which have a little more of a 19th-century appearance than some of the alternatives.

Chapter titles, page headers, and footers are in Baskerville (what else can one use for a Holmes story?), and the decorative drop caps are in Romantique, which preserves the feel of the *Strand*'s original drop caps.

The punctuation is carried out according to the rules apparently followed by the *Strand*'s typesetters. These include extra spacing after full stops (periods), thin spaces following opening quotation marks, and extra spaces on either side of punctuation such as question marks, exclamation marks and semi-colons. This seems to allow the type to breathe more easily, especially in long spoken and quoted exchanges, and we have therefore adopted this style here.

Some of the orthography has also been deliberately changed to match the original—for instance, " Baker Street" has become " Baker-street" throughout.

THE AUTHOR

 UGH ASHTON was born in the United Kingdom, and moved to Japan in 1988, living in the historic town of Kamakura, a little to the south of Yokohama with his wife, Yoshiko, before returning to live in Lichfield in 2016.

He is best known for his Sherlock Holmes stories, which have been hailed as some of the most authentic pastiches on the market, and have received favourable reviews from Sherlockians and non-Sherlockians alike.

More about Hugh Ashton and his books may be found at:

http://HughAshtonBooks.info

and he may be contacted at:

hashton@mac.com

Lightning Source UK Ltd.
Milton Keynes UK
UKHW020635260821
389510UK00009B/332